LOOK OUT FOR THE WHOLE SERIES!

D0503385

THE CASE OF THE SURFER DUDE
WHO'S TRULY RUDE

Hodder
Children's
Books

A division of Hachette Children's Books

**Special thanks to Lucy Courtenay
and Artful Doodlers**

Copyright © 2009 Chorion Rights Limited, a Chorion company

First published in Great Britain in 2009 by Hodder Children's Books

1

A Catalogue record for this book is available from the British Library

ISBN 978 0 340 98116 0

Typeset in Weiss by Avon DataSet Ltd,
Bidford on Avon, Warwickshire

Printed in Great Britain by
Clays Ltd, St Ives plc

The paper and board used in this paperback by Hodder Children's
Books are natural recyclable products made from wood grown in
sustainable forests. The manufacturing processes conform to the
environmental regulations of the country of origin.

Hodder Children's Books
a division of Hachette Children's Books
338 Euston Road, London NW1 3BH
An Hachette Livre UK Company
www.hachettelivre.co.uk

Chapter One

The golden beach stretched for miles. The azure sea lapped the shore. A row of low-slung wooden beach houses followed the coastline, their verandas and balconies opening straight out on to the sand. A blue heat haze hung over the heath-covered foothills in the distance. England? No way. *This* was Californ-I-A.

On a marked-out volleyball pitch in the sand, the four Kirrin cousins took their places: Allie and Dylan on one side, and Jo and Max on the other.

"I have to say, these teams don't seem fair," Jo grinned, tossing the ball from hand to hand as she stared down her cousins – one blond, one dark – on the far side of the net. "Max and I are much better volleyball players than you two."

Dylan looked humble. "Oh well," he sighed, winking at Allie. "We'll do the best we can. Go ahead and serve."

Jo shrugged and served the ball.

Dylan raced to the net. He set the ball up to Allie. Allie leaped into the air like a blond-haired kangaroo and spiked the ball so ferociously that both Jo and Max were knocked off their feet.

"Oopphh!" Jo groaned, landing on her bum.

"Ohhhh!" Max mumbled. He was a little more muffled than Jo, as he had ended up with his chin in the sand.

"Rowfff," whined Timmy, Jo's dog, covering his handsome black and tan eyebrows with his paws.

"Boo-yow!" Allie crowed. She gave Dylan a victorious high-five and tossed her blond hair back over her shoulders. "This is Malibu *beach* volleyball! You're on *my* turf now."

Max sat up and spat out what looked like half the beach. "It's worth a mouthful of sand to be in Malibu," he grinned up at Allie, pushing his tousled blond fringe out of his eyes. "It was great of your parents to invite us."

Jo's parents Ravi and George came down the steps of the beach house to join the kids.

"Too bad your mother had to go to a Kwakiutl tribal art conference, Allie," said Jo's father Ravi. "They make masks that look like *this*." He started pulling hideous mask-like faces at the kids, making Jo groan with embarrassment.

"But if her absence means Ravi and I have to bring you kids to Paradise for a few weeks, well," George cut in with a grin, "as parents we make sacrifices."

Ravi stopped making faces long enough to rummage in his rucksack and produce a camera. He waved it at Jo and the others in excitement. "I'm going to Hollywood to spot movie stars!" he announced. Malibu wasn't far down the Californian coast from Beverly Hills. "I want to see the twitchy guy from the comedies who makes those faces."

"And I'm off to collect local algae, fungi and moulds," said George, patting her samples bag fondly.

Jo rolled her eyes. "Go wild, Mum," she teased.

Max pointed reverently towards a colourful run-down beach shack that had been built right into the hills behind it. Surfboards and beach bums leaned up against its walls. "I want to go *there*," he said. "Duke's Surf Shack! It's in all the surfing magazines. All the best surfers hang there." Shading his eyes, Max looked out towards the ocean. "Look who's on the water right now!"

The others squinted out to sea. They could see a couple of specks riding the waves, but for all they knew they could have been looking at seals.

"That's Bodhi Weinrib," Max gasped, pointing at the tousled blond speck that was leading the way. "And Jeannie Garcia. And Big Steve and Little Steve Renfro. They're awesome!"

Now the others had some names to go on, the specks started looking like humans on slick-looking boards. They curved up, over and under the curling waves.

"They do seem pretty good," Dylan said, impressed.

Suddenly, the surfers' boards all appeared to splinter into pieces. The surfers were hurled through the air, skidding gracelessly and landing on their noses in the water.

"I take it back," said Dylan.

Max frowned. The surfers were being swept in to shore, dangerously close to the pilings of a pier that jutted out into the sea. "Something's wrong," he said. "They're in trouble!"

Chapter Two

The cousins raced down the beach and plunged into the waves. The hapless surfers were struggling with the currents. All were in danger of being smashed against the pilings that held the pier in place.

Max splashed towards the shaggy-haired blond surfer he'd identified to the others as Bodhi Weinrib. He grabbed a shattered piece of surfboard as it floated by. Then he seized Bodhi by the scruff of his wetsuit and pulled him up on to the board.

"Ooff," Bodhi groaned.

Max held Bodhi firmly in place. He steered the

broken board away from the pilings, then let the waves carry him and his passenger safely in to shore.

Allie, Dylan, Jo and Timmy weren't far behind. They were towing, helping or barking at the remaining surfers, coaxing them out of the danger zone and ashore.

Bodhi gasped and retched on the sand. He squinted up at Max. "Thanks, bro," he croaked. "Don't know what happened out there . . ."

A relaxed-looking Hawaiian man in his fifties with a tan to rival a leather saddle had been watching the whole thing.

"Good job, little grommets," he said in a gravelly drawl, patting the Kirrins on the back. "You saved the best prospects for my team."

He glanced around. One of his surfers was cradling an injured arm. Two others were now limping away up the beach. The man scratched his head. "But seems they're all banged up," he said ruefully. "So now I've got *no* prospects."

Bodhi struggled to his feet. "Still got *me*, Duke," he said weakly.

Max's eyes widened. "You're Duke Sonoma?"

he gasped. "*The* Duke Sonoma?" He spun round to his cousins. "Duke sponsors a team every year in the Pacific West Pro-Am," he explained enthusiastically. "It's, like, *the* team to be on."

Duke grinned. "You handled that busted board pretty good," he told Max. "Try-outs are later today, if you're interested."

Bodhi nodded. His nose was peeling from too much sun, sea and surf. "You should try out, bro," he agreed. "I am. The team hangs out at Duke's place during the tournament. Most cool."

"You can borrow a board from the shop," Duke told Max.

Dylan picked up the broken pieces of surfboard as they washed ashore. "Bodhi's going to need a new board too," he said. He waved the bits in the air. "Unless we can just lick the pieces of this and stick it back together . . ."

Duke invited the Five plus Bodhi back to his surf shack. The shop was just as exciting inside as it looked from the outside. The walls were plastered with old surfing posters. Shelves groaned with trophies and tropical knick-knacks like dried puffer fish and driftwood. A huge conch shell lay on the counter.

Max was particularly interested in the row of surfboards lined up against one wall.

"Sometimes we get shore breaks round here," Bodhi said, looking at the boards with Max. "Watch out for those – they'll mess you up."

"Speaking of breaks," said Jo, studying what remained of Bodhi's surfboard, "there's something very wrong with your board . . ."

Allie picked up a glass of water from the counter, dumped the water in a potted plant and used the bottom of the glass to get a close-up of the damage.

"Wow," she said. "There's a ton of tiny little holes drilled in the board."

The others clustered around for a look. Max gazed through the glass at pieces of all the different boards that had shattered out on the waves that day. The magnification showed rows of dots that differed very slightly in colour.

"Same with these boards," Max said. "The holes are covered with resin to hide them, but they're there." He turned to Bodhi, who was listening with his mouth open. "Your board broke along the drill line."

"Somebody sabotaged your boards," Dylan said. "Why would they do that?"

Bodhi pulled himself together. He wasn't used to being in the same room as a bunch of amateur sleuths. "Massive competition to get on Duke's team, bro," he said with a shrug. "Maybe someone's trying to improve his odds."

"Don't worry," said Jo in determination. "We'll work it out."

"I'll be in the try-outs," Max put in. "I can check things out from the inside."

Jo picked up a flyer from a stack on the counter. She turned it over, and smiled. "There's an Extreme Sand Sculpture contest this week . . ." she said.

"We could enter it and keep an eye on things on the beach," Dylan said promptly. "I'll probably get sand down my shorts, but it'll be worth it."

"Getting 'bro-active', huh?" Bodhi said, with an amused snort. "I like it! Go get 'em!"

He slapped Dylan on the back. Taken by surprise, Dylan stumbled backwards into a surfboard leaning against the wall.

"Ooppphh," he said, watching in dismay as the board fell on to another board, which fell on to another board – all the way around the shack.

"And I can stay and clean up here," said Allie loudly. The falling surfboards made a heck of a racket. "See if anything looks suspicious."

The last board toppled over and caught Allie smartly on the head.

"Owww," she wailed, rubbing her head. "Like that . . ."

Chapter Three

Jo had a feeling she was going to enjoy Extreme Sand Sculpture.

She caught her breath and wiped her hands on her shorts, straightening up from the deep hole she had been digging just in time to catch a spadeful of sand in the face. It buried her up to her knees.

"Ahhhhhh!"

A few metres away, Dylan was digging like a hungry dog after a bone. Sand was flying everywhere. Mostly over Jo.

"Dylan – watch it!" Jo spluttered, burrowing her way out of the sand. "What are you *doing*?!"

"Making the base for our sculpture of John D.

Rockefeller," Dylan panted. He threw another enormous spadeful of sand in Jo's direction. "He was the world's first billionaire."

"I don't *want* to do a sculpture of a billionaire," Jo said.

Dylan sighed. "All right," he said, "we'll do Howard Hughes. He was worth a bundle."

Jo shook her head. All Dylan ever thought about was getting rich. "I don't care about money," she told him.

Dylan steadied himself on his spade. "Take a deep breath," he advised, sounding in need of a deep breath himself. "You don't know what you're saying."

"It doesn't matter what we make," Jo said impatiently. "The point of this is to keep an eye on the surfing try-outs."

Dylan nodded. "Then let's do a billionaire," he said.

"You do what you want," Jo said. "I'll make my own sculpture, and it'll be better than whatever you make."

Jo and Dylan narrowed their eyes at each other. The smell of competition coursed through the air. It smelled very like damp sand.

"Go!" Dylan shouted, and whirled back to his digging with even more fury than before.

Jo clicked her fingers. "Timmy!"

Timmy threw himself into digging the hole Jo had started, throwing even more sand Dylan's way.

"Heyyyyyy!" Dylan shouted.

Back at Duke's surf shack, Max, Allie and Bodhi were preparing to leave. The mess had been a little tricky to fix, but they'd managed to get all the surfboards back into what they hoped was the right order.

"Did anybody have access to your board when you weren't around?" Max asked Bodhi as they stepped out on to the sand and looked up and down the beach.

Bodhi pointed to the outside wall of the shack. "It was leaning on that wall," he said. "Lots of people could've tweaked it. But such a person would be no bro, bro."

A thirteen-year-old girl was mincing up the beach towards them. It didn't take much to work out that the bikini she was wearing was an expensive one.

14

"Bodhi!" she called in a breathless, girly voice, clutching a box to her chest. "Bodhi, Bodhi, Bodhi!"

"Yuck – Sierra Richmond," Allie muttered to Max. "Meanest girl in school. She makes the Dunston twins look like golden rays of sunshine."

The Dunstons were the Kirrins' sworn enemies back in Falcongate. Max winced.

"Allie?" said Sierra, stopping in front of Allie and looking her up and down. "What are *you* doing here? The losers' beach is down that way."

"And good morning to you, Sierra," Allie said politely.

Sierra tossed her hair and turned her back on Allie and Max. "I'm Sierra," she told Bodhi, fixing him with a terrifying smile. "I saw you pretending not to notice me at the Lobster Festival, and I could tell you like lobster, so I brought you one."

She gave Bodhi the box. Sure enough, it contained a lobster.

Allie leaned over the box. "Don't worry, little guy," she said. "Getting dunked in butter beats hanging out with Sierra."

Sierra gave Allie a death stare. Turning to Bodhi, she fixed her smile back in place. "I'm trying out for

15

Duke's little surf team too, Bodhi," she said, and linked arms with him. "Wouldn't it be cute if we end up on the team together?"

"All of humanity is on the same team," said Bodhi, waving vaguely in the air. "And we're riding one big wave." He looked at Max. "C'mon, bro – let's jet."

Max didn't need to be asked twice. He seized his board and hurried into the surf after the shaggy blond surfer.

"Bodhi!" Sierra trilled. "Wait for me . . . !" Grabbing a surfboard, she wiggled off after the boys.

The atmosphere at the beach started to soar as the time for Duke's Pro-Am team try-outs approached. Allie leaned back against the shack and enjoyed the feel of hot sun on her skin. She noticed an elegant, older woman walking down the beach.

The woman looked out of place among the sunburned teenagers. Slung over her arm was a gym bag with a logo showing someone doing yoga. She grimaced as a passing surfer kicked sand over her expensive shoes.

"Careful with my shoes!" she called angrily. "They're worth more than the average house! I'll sue you if I have to!"

She turned and looked at Allie. "You're not Duke," she said, rather unnecessarily. "Where's Duke?"

Duke stepped out of the shack. "Arlene Gundall," he said. He sounded wary. "Don't s'pose you want to rent a belly-board?"

Arlene's smile reminded Allie of a shark. "Look, Dukey," she said, "we both know I'm going to buy your little rat-shack here when you can't pay the mortgage."

"I'll pay," Duke insisted. "I always make good money with my Pro-Am team."

Arlene smirked. "You think so?" she said. "That's cute. Face it – two months from now, I'm building my mansion here." She looked around. "This spot will be perfect for my yoga room . . ."

Allie couldn't stand by and let this woman talk to Duke as if he was a piece of dirt on her beach towel. "Duke will raise the money," she said fiercely. Arlene and Duke both turned and looked at her in surprise. "I bet this year's Pro-Am team is his best ever . . ."

17

She turned and looked out to sea. It was time for the try-outs.

Chapter Four

Out on the ocean, Max, Bodhi and the other surfers sat patiently on their boards. They could feel the swell. Some good waves were heading their way. This was their big chance to make it – or wipe out.

"Choose a strong wave, Bro-Diddley," Bodhi advised Max as he lay down on his board and started paddling. "Make it count."

Max turned his board and started paddling out further, beyond where the waves were starting to break. He got the fright of his life when a familiar head, wearing a diving mask and snorkel, popped out of the water in front of him.

"Whooooah!" he yelled, almost falling off his board in shock.

George pulled her mask up and unplugged the snorkel in her mouth. "Oh, hello Max," she said cheerfully. She waved some wet green fronds at him. "Just collecting seaweed. You know – I get by with a little kelp from my friends!" She roared with laughter at her own joke. "Good luck surfing!"

With a deep breath, Max's aunt disappeared beneath the surface again.

Bodhi, Sierra and another girl, called Otter, had all caught a wave. They were riding it expertly in to the shore. Max watched as they cruised smoothly to a halt on the sand. Bodhi gave Otter a high-five, paying no attention to Sierra as the girl hugged him tightly from behind.

"We were great, Bodhi," Max could hear Sierra boasting. "It was an honour for the others to be in the same ocean as us."

Bodhi looked perplexed at Sierra's attention. "Er – whatever," he said politely. He looked back at the ocean. "Check out the others . . ."

Three other surfers had caught a wave. But this time, they wiped out spectacularly, somersaulting through the air. Their boards snapped into pieces. Debris was hurled across the waves. Several other surfers ducked, for fear of getting half a board in the back.

"Oh, no – they've been sabotaged again!" Allie gasped, from where she had been watching the try-outs on the beach with Dylan, Jo and Timmy. "Let's find their boards!"

Back in the sea, Max noticed that he had company again. A whiskery-faced harbour seal had poked its head above the waves and was gazing at him with round brown eyes.

"Oh – hello," said Max, charmed. "You look like a friendly little seal . . ."

The seal barked in agreement, but then it leaped out of the water and slapped Max around the face with its flippers.

"Ahhh," Max said, rubbing his face and feeling a little shocked. "I guess California seals are more in-your-face than English ones. Literally."

The seal re-surfaced and barked at Max again.

"I don't know what your problem is," said Max, "but I have a wave to catch."

Waving at the seal, he paddled energetically

towards a big swell, catching it just as it broke.

"Wayyyyyyyy!" he yelled in exhilaration, feeling the speed of the wave towing him in to the shore.

"Go Max, whooo!" Allie cheered from the beach.

"Yay!" screamed Dylan and Jo. "Whoooo!"

Max felt as though he was on top of the world. He performed a few slick moves, then rode back over the crest of the wave and settled down on the still water again. This was far too much fun to head for shore just yet.

Now a dolphin joined him. It chattered happily, poking its smooth grey nose out of the blue water.

"Hello to you, too," Max grinned. He could get used to the wildlife in this place.

The dolphin leaped out of the water in a graceful arc. It landed its whole weight on the front of Max's board. Max was catapulted off, straight towards the shore.

"Waaaaagh!" he yelled, flailing through the air.

There was nothing he could do. He saw the shocked faces of the surfers gathered on the sand as he landed smack on top of Duke Sonoma himself.

"Awaahh!" Duke yelled, and collapsed under Max's weight.

Groggily, Max shook his head to clear it.

"OK," said Duke from somewhere underneath him. "I got my team. Bodhi, Otter, and this guy who's sitting on me. Sierra – you're first back-up."

Bodhi and Otter ran to help Max and Duke back on to their feet. Everyone exchanged high-fives. They'd made Duke's famous Pro-Am team! Everyone except Sierra, that was. She simmered in fury a little to one side.

Allie, Jo, Dylan and Timmy ran up to join the party. They were dragging the pieces of broken surfboard that they'd rescued when the three surfers before Max had wiped out.

"Sorry to be a wet blanket," Jo said, "but look at these boards – they've been drilled through . . ."

Everyone stared. The evidence was right before their eyes. The boards had been deliberately ruined before their riders had even stepped into the sea.

"Somebody around here doesn't like surfboards," Dylan concluded.

"More like somebody around here doesn't like Duke," said Allie, looking upset. "I'm sorry, Duke, but someone's trying to sabotage your team."

Chapter Five

Down at the beach a little later on, Dylan put the finishing touches to his sand sculpture of the Leaning Tower of Pisa. It was a work of art.

Nearby, Jo filled a wheelbarrow with sand, measured out a little water and tipped it in to the mix. Max and Allie watched.

"I still don't get it," said Jo, stirring her sand mixture. "Why would someone want to sabotage Duke's team?"

Dylan flicked a couple of tiny grains of sand off his Leaning Tower's top storey. "Maybe Duke has enemies," he suggested

"He saved his entire Peace Corps unit from a

forest fire," Max pointed out. "He gives money to charity to buy poor kids Christmas presents."

Duke Sonoma sounded like a seriously nice person.

"OK," Dylan admitted. "Unless a kid got, say, spinach for Christmas, Duke shouldn't have any enemies."

"Maybe someone wants Duke's shack," Allie said, gazing up the beach to where the old surf shack leaned in to the hillside behind it. "That Arlene woman who was here earlier? She's going to buy his place if he can't pay his mortgage."

Jo's mind whirred into action. "And if he doesn't have a team, he won't make any money," she said thoughtfully. "Sounds like a motive to me. I say we check her out."

Dylan looked surprised. He pointed at Jo's mound of sand. "Don't you want to finish your sculpture first?" he asked.

Jo shrugged. "It *is* finished. It's a mound."

It certainly was a mound. It was round, and generally moundish.

"It looks like a giant sand pimple," said Dylan crossly. It felt as if Jo had cheated somehow.

"My sculpture is daring, it's imaginative . . ."

A seagull fluttered down and landed on the Leaning Tower. The whole sculpture crumbled away, covering Timmy in sand. Timmy gave a muffled woof.

Jo grinned at Dylan's face. "Now it's a mound like mine," she said. "Only mine will last, because it's the right mixture of sand and water. Now, let's go and find Arlene."

Jo strode off. Max and Dylan hurried after her.

"She was carrying a yoga bag, and she didn't come by car," said Allie, catching up with Jo."She must have been walking to or from a yoga class."

"I'll check online," Dylan said. "See if there are any yoga classes in walking distance ..."

Timmy emerged from what was left of Dylan's creation. He shook himself off. Sand sprayed everywhere.

"Oh Dylan, your mound is *ruined*," Jo teased.

A yoga class was taking place on the beach later that afternoon. The Five found six people, including Arlene, Bodhi and Sierra, doing the class. They were led by an impossibly bendy instructor.

27

In the middle of a stretch, Arlene was talking on her mobile phone.

". . . you know those beautiful trees on the hill above where the kitchen will be? Cut 'em down – I want to park the four-wheel drive there."

Allie settled down beside Arlene and adopted a lotus pose in the sand. "Hi, Ms Gundall," she said breezily. "Isn't yoga class great? So serene, so centring, so restful . . ."

Jo leaned in. "How come you're sabotaging Duke?" she asked bluntly. "You won't get away with it."

Dylan was attempting to put his foot up behind his neck. "We know you don't want him to make the money for his mortgage," he panted. "So you're trying to sabotage his team." He struggled for a moment. His foot was somewhere behind his ear. "All right, I'm stuck . . ."

"Who cares if he wins?" said Arlene smoothly. She stretched to the side. "I have powerful friends – they'll say his shack needs so many safety improvements that he can't possibly afford them."

"But, then he'll lose the place!" Max gasped.

"That's the idea," Arlene purred. "Win or lose,

28

Duke's out on his rear end." She inhaled and closed her eyes. "And, cleansing breath ..."

The Kirrins looked at each other in disappointment.

"So much for *her* motive," said Jo to the others in a low voice. "I think we can scratch Arlene off the suspect list."

The yoga instructor now shifted into a different position. Bodhi changed his position comfortably, but Sierra looked like she was struggling.

"This position's a little difficult – oh, I'm falling!" she gasped theatrically, making sure she was toppling towards her target. "Help me, Bodhi! Woahhhh . . ."

She tried to snuggle against the surfer as he helped her up. "Thanks, Bodhi," she said coyly, flirting with him. "You're so much better at this than I am. You're good at everything."

"Sure," said Bodhi, hardly listening as he settled back into position. "Whatever."

Sierra plopped down comfortably in the sand. Ignoring the instructor now, she sipped some water from a sports bottle and started filing her nails.

"She's not doing any of the stretches," Jo said

indignantly. "That's cheating."

"She cheats a lot," Allie muttered. "I think she pays someone to do her schoolwork."

Max brightened. "Hey, wait a minute!" he said. "Maybe she's cheating at surfing, too!"

Dylan was still trying to get himself out of his leg tangle. "You mean, she's not sabotaging boards to stop the team, but to make sure she gets on the team," he said, his face pressed down into the sand. He gave a violent lurch to free himself, but got more tangled than ever.

"So she messed with people's boards," said Jo, thinking through Max's theory, "so she'd get on the team with Bodhi. She obviously has a crush on him."

"But why would she sabotage *Bodhi's* board?" Allie pointed out.

"To keep suspicion off her," Max said promptly. "She did it during practice, not during the try-outs. So it didn't hurt his chances of making the team."

"Well," said Allie, "the team's practising this afternoon, and she's still the back-up. Let's keep an eye on her."

Dylan finally unwound himself. Exhausted,

he collapsed into the sand. "Ooohhh – oopphh," he groaned.

The yoga instructor changed position again. The class followed suit.

"Hey," said Jo, grinning. "Timmy's better at yoga than Dylan."

Timmy was stretching beautifully, giving happy little pants.

"That's the 'Downward Dog' position," Dylan pointed out grumpily. "Of course he's better at it . . ."

Chapter Six

Back on the beach the next day, Jo and Dylan got on with their next attempts at Extreme Sand Sculpture. This time, Jo was shaping a pile of sand into a low circle. Nearby, Dylan had surpassed his Leaning Tower of Pisa with a miniature Eiffel Tower. However, no sooner had Dylan stuck a little paper flag in the top than the whole thing fell down. Sighing, he started again.

Jo had started again too. She'd really pushed the boat out his time, and was working on a long, low rectangle of sand. Refusing to be defeated by technical impossibilities, Dylan finished a miniature Mount Rushmore. It too collapsed.

When Jo had finished a long, horizontal tube of sand, and Dylan's fabulous retro, finned rocket-ship had gone the same way as the Eiffel Tower and Mount Rushmore, Dylan threw his hands up in defeat.

"It seems I'm not strong on engineering," he sighed despondently.

Jo regarded her long, neat row of geometric shapes. "And I'm about as creative as . . . as . . . See – I can't even think of anything," she said, sounding a little sad.

"You build stuff that lasts," Dylan said. "I design stuff worth looking at." He raised his eyebrows at his cousin. "Maybe it's time for a merger?"

Jo nodded, pleased with the idea. "Who knows what we can come up with if we work together?" she said.

They spent the rest of the morning and half the afternoon in happy silence, working side by side. A magnificent living room made entirely of sand started to take shape. Monsters like werewolves and vampires lounged about on enormous sand sofas. A tall, Frankenstein figure posed as a butler, standing ready with a serving tray and towering above everyone who passed. Timmy eyed the werewolf cautiously, sniffed it, and gave it a wide berth for the rest of the afternoon.

The Pro-Am team were heading out into the surf to practise their moves. Allie was right behind them.

"Whoa – scary!" Max said approvingly, stopping to admire his cousins' handiwork.

"We call it 'Crazy Creature Club'," Jo explained. "They're creatures . . . kind of crazy . . . and they look like they're in a club . . ."

Sierra snorted. "That's lame," she said unkindly. She turned to Bodhi. "Don't you think that's lame, Bodhi?"

Bodhi ignored the question. He was examining the bottom of his board. "No drill holes in my board. Skeg's good," he declared, referring to the fin on the bottom of his board. "How 'bout you, Bro-do Baggins?"

Max checked the bottom of his board. "Mine's clean."

Satisfied, Bodhi led the team out into the water. Sierra stayed as close to Bodhi as she could, without stepping on his heels. Dylan settled down on the giant sand sofa and pulled out a pair of binoculars. There was a great view from here.

As Bodhi, Sierra and Otter paddled into a wave and took off towards the shore, Max turned his board and paddled in a slightly different direction. He caught another wave, stood up and started practising his turns. But halfway through, he looked down – and noticed that the back end of his board was drooping like a deflated balloon. The surfboard tipped backwards dangerously. Max scurried to the front, trying to keep his balance.

"Max is in trouble!" said Dylan, sitting up and pressing his binoculars more firmly to his eyes. "There's something wrong with his board!"

Jo shaded her eyes and looked out to sea. "He's OK," she said at last. "He's riding it."

Max had got the board back under control. But his moves were messed up. It was all he could do to aim the wilting board at the shore and hope he'd land up on the sand. Up on shore, Sierra had already landed. She had picked up her board and was hurrying up to Duke's surf shack.

The seal who'd slapped Max the day before made a second appearance. It barked at Max in a friendly manner.

"You again?" Max asked, glancing sideways. "Come to apologise?"

The seal jumped out of the water and knocked him off the board.

"Ooophh," Max gasped, splashing down into the water. "Clearly not . . ."

He reached up and grabbed what was left of his board. Now the dolphin popped up.

"Hey, Mr Dolphin," said Max hopefully. "How about a lift?"

The dolphin appeared to nod. Greatly relieved, Max grabbed on to its fin with his free hand. The dolphin started towing Max towards the shore. It began picking up speed.

"Going a little fast there . . . a little too fast . . ." Max shouted, hanging on like grim death. "I think you should slow—"

As if it had understood, the dolphin stopped abruptly. For the second time in as many days, Max was catapulted through the air and on to the beach. He landed on the sand, face first.

". . . woahhhh – down," he finished weakly, spitting out sand.

Jo ran over to retrieve what was left of Max's surfboard. It looked like the saboteur had just struck again.

"Are you sure you checked your board before you went out?" Jo asked, coming back with the damaged board as Allie, Dylan and Bodhi helped Max up.

Max took his board and checked it again. "The foam core's all melted," he said in surprise, feeling the foam at the back of the board squidging between his fingers. He sniffed it. "Citrus solvent.

Somebody could have injected it into the board – that would dissolve the foam."

"And it smells lemony fresh," Dylan put in with a grin.

Jo examined Max's skeg, and prised away a small, heart-shaped pendant.

"I recognise that pendant," said Allie. "It belongs to Sierra."

The Five hadn't seen Sierra walking carefully towards them from Duke's surf shack. She was carrying a cake bearing an image of Bodhi's face on the icing.

"Sierra?" said Bodhi, not realising Sierra was just behind him. "She's that chick who keeps bugging me, right? She's bad news . . ."

Sierra's face dropped. She let the cake fall into the sand and hurried away, her face flaming scarlet.

Chapter Seven

Still talking about how and why Sierra could have planted her pendant on Max's ruined board, the Five walked into Duke's surf shack. Bodhi had disappeared.

"And it's OK to snoop in Sierra's locker?" Allie checked, as they stopped beside a wall of four metal lockers: one for each member of Duke's new Pro-Am team.

Max nodded. "Yes, Duke lets the team use them during the tournament. They're not private or anything."

Dylan scanned along the lockers, which were marked with photos of the team members.

When he reached Sierra's, he tried the door. It wasn't locked.

If the Five had needed any more evidence of Sierra's crush on Bodhi, they'd found it. On the inside of the door, a photo of Sierra had been stuck next to a photo of Bodhi. A heart had been cut out of paper, and pasted above the photos. But it was the contents of the locker itself that interested the Five. They included jars of liquid resin, jars of paint, a small drill and several drill bits, and a container of citrus solvent.

"Drills, resin," Dylan murmured, sorting through the incriminating evidence. "She couldn't be more red-handed if she wore gloves made of strawberry jam."

"Well, she's supposed to be coming here tonight for the big *luau* Duke's having . . ." Max said. The Five had been invited to the special Hawaiian-style beach party being held for the surfers.

Jo shook her head. "We have to find her before that," she said.

"Found her," said Allie.

Sierra had appeared in the doorway. Dylan slammed the locker shut guiltily.

"Sierra," Allie began as Sierra gave them all a hostile stare. "We need to talk to you."

Sierra's eyes filled with tears. "Well, *I* don't want to talk to *you*," she snapped.

She turned and fled. The Kirrins looked at each other, then shot off in hot pursuit with Timmy at Jo's heels.

Sierra had swerved off the beach. She was now running up a path into the foothills that backed on to the ocean. The Five kept up the chase. Checking over her shoulder, Sierra didn't see a sudden bend in the path. She lost her footing and stumbled, sliding down the hill and into a gully.

"Woahhhhh!" she screamed, trying to catch her balance.

The Five raced to the edge of the gully. Jo's eyes widened.

"Sierra – don't move!" she yelled.

Sierra had disturbed a sleeping rattlesnake. The bad-tempered reptile rattled its tail and curled up, ready for a deadly strike. Bending down, Jo seized a rock. She threw it hard at the ground in front of the snake. The rock startled the rattler, and it retreated into the undergrowth.

41

"Can I move now?" said Sierra, looking white with terror.

The Five slithered down the gully towards the girl. They almost felt sorry for her.

"Sure," said Dylan, sliding to a halt beside Sierra. "If you'll tell us why you sabotaged Max's board?"

Sierra looked shocked. "I didn't do anything to anybody's surfboard," she protested.

"Then how come you ran from us?" Jo demanded.

Sierra's shoulders slumped. "I didn't want anybody to know Bodhi blew me off," she muttered. "Even after I gave him my heart pendant."

"Wait!" said Max. He fumbled in his pocket and pulled out the pendant. "This pendant?"

"Yeah," Sierra sniffed. "He just said, 'Whatever, bro,' and stuck it in his pocket." She frowned. "Where did you get it?"

"Off the skeg of my board," Max said. His brain fired up as a new solution to the puzzle of the saboteur sprang into his head. "I think Bodhi put it there."

"Then he must have put the drills and resin

and stuff in Sierra's locker, to make her look guilty," Jo guessed.

"So *Bodhi's* been the cheat all along?" said Dylan in surprise. "Why would he sabotage his own board?"

"He had to," Allie said. "Would've looked pretty suspicious if his was the only one untouched."

Jo jumped up. "Let's go and find him," she said at once. "Allie, you check at Duke's. Max, you try the pier. Dylan and I can try the yoghurt stand."

Sierra pouted. She hated being left out. "What should *I* do?" she whined.

Jo looked down at Sierra's bare feet. "Go home and put on some calamine lotion," she advised. "You're standing in poison ivy."

Allie left the others at the yoghurt stand and the pier and headed on to Duke's surf shack alone. She entered and gazed around. It was deserted.

"Duke?" she checked, peering around the room. "Hello? Anybody?"

She noticed one of Duke's surf posters on the back wall of the shack. The picture showed surfers in the water, with a lighthouse in the background.

But the light in the lighthouse actually seemed to be *moving*.

Pictures weren't supposed to move. Allie crossed the room to check out the poster more closely. With her head on one side, she tried to make sense of what she was seeing. Then, experimentally, she lifted the corner of the poster and peered behind it.

There was a large hole in the wall. And beyond the hole, Allie saw a tunnel leading into the hillside behind the shack.

Wasting no time, Allie scrambled up and wriggled in. The tunnel was short and sandy. Within moments, Allie had crawled along it, emerging into a huge cavern – *inside the hill*.

Then she gasped at the object standing in the centre of the cavern itself. The hulk of an ancient Spanish galleon lay partially sunk into the cavern's mud floor.

"Wow!" Allie muttered, staring at the old ship. "I mean, *way* wow."

The beam of a torch flashed in the darkness. It was the light Allie had seen behind the poster. Bodhi was standing on the main deck of the galleon, a torch tucked under his arm, stacking heavy wooden crates. He hadn't seen her yet.

Allie crawled carefully out of the tunnel. She let herself down silently on to the galleon's quarterdeck, took a step forward – and felt herself falling. The deck had collapsed beneath her weight.

Allie plunged through the hole, her arms flailing. She squelched down into the mud beneath the rotten decking, right up to her waist. Panicking now, she wriggled. The mud held her fast.

Taking slow, measured steps, Bodhi made his way over. He shone his torch at Allie. "Well,

well," he murmured. "Looks like somebody wiped out." He gave Allie an unfriendly smile. "You are *most* busted . . ."

Chapter Eight

The more Allie struggled, the deeper she sank into the mud. She was well and truly stuck.

Bodhi grinned, and continued carrying the wooden crates up on to the quarterdeck. "Kind of a drag you found me, girl-bro," he said over his shoulder. "I don't really feel like sharing this."

"What is it?" Allie asked, curiosity overcoming panic for a few moments.

"Gold," Bodhi smirked. "My grandfather heard about this shipwreck, loaded with it."

Allie gasped. Gold! "How'd it get *here?*" she asked.

"Ran aground in a storm," Bodhi said, shaking his

head. "Drag. Then it got buried in a mudslide before they got the gold off. *Double* drag."

Allie glared at the surfer as he headed past her to collect another crate. He was almost finished. "And you cheated to get on Duke's team, so you could hang around his shack all you wanted," she said, working it out. "So you could dig that tunnel."

Bodhi dusted off his hands. "Bro, you're like Sherlock *Bromes*," he said admiringly. "Too bad you won't be able to brag to anybody. You're kinda stuck in that hole, am I right?"

"I can't budge," Allie complained.

Bodhi raised his shaggy blond eyebrows. "Got a cell phone on you?"

Allie felt a wave of relief. Bodhi was going to let her make a call! "In my pants pocket," she said, looking down at the mud. "I can't reach it."

"Good," Bodhi grinned. "Then I can leave you there forever."

Allie's heart sank. So much for *that* idea.

"Well," Bodhi said breezily, "time to get the gold to my van." He hefted the top crate into his arms and headed towards the mouth of the tunnel. Miserably, Allie watched him go.

"Don't go anywhere," Bodhi said over his shoulder, staggering at the weight of the gold in the crate. "Heh-heh!" he laughed, pleased with himself. "Hey Bodhi – you're funny . . ."

He pushed and shoved the crate down the tunnel, jumped lightly down on to the shack floor and picked it up again. Checking that no one was hanging around, he then hurried away up the beach.

Just as Bodhi disappeared from sight with his booty, the others started gathering on the far side of the shack.

"No sign of him at the pier," Max panted.

"He wasn't at the yoghurt stand either," Dylan said. "And to make matters worse, they were out of crushed cookie yoghurt."

They walked past the open door of the surf shack and peered inside.

"Hmm, no Allie," said Jo in surprise. "Maybe she's back at the house . . ."

Poor Allie was nowhere near the house. She was still wedged in the hole in the old galleon's deck.

49

She didn't dare struggle too much. She couldn't risk sinking any further.

Looking round the cavern, she saw a length of broken plank just within reach. Pulling the plank towards her, she used it to reach a coil of rope lying a little further away. Panting with the effort, Allie pulled the rope towards her with the broken end of the plank. At last, the end was within reach. She coiled it up quickly. She wanted the grappling hook tied to the far end.

When she had the grappling hook, she eyed the mouth of the tunnel. Then she whirled the rope over her head a couple of times. "I hope this isn't as hard as it looks . . ." she muttered to herself. If she could just get through to the shack – if the hook could just land on the object she wanted . . .

Chapter Nine

The grappling hook whistled through the air, dragging the rope with it. It flew down the tunnel, pushed past the poster and landed directly on the old conch shell that stood on the surf shack counter. Just as Allie had planned, the sharp end of the hook caught round the edge of the shell. She pulled the rope back slowly and steadily until the conch was in her hands.

"Huh," she said, handling the conch in delight. "I guess I'm pretty good at it."

Putting the conch shell to her mouth, she took a deep breath and blew. The shell produced a low throbbing sound, like a foghorn. It boomed round the cavern and – she hoped – as far as the beach beyond.

Jo, Dylan, Max and Timmy headed on towards their beach house. As they reached Jo and Dylan's Crazy Creature Club sand sculpture, Timmy pricked up his ears. He barked urgently, then turned and raced back to the surf shack. Puzzled, the others looked at each other. Then they began to run as well.

Timmy was racing. It was hard to keep up with him across the soft sand. When he reached Duke's surf shack he skidded to a halt, and waited.

The sound of the conch was unmissable in here. The cousins poked around the walls, listening. Where was it coming from?

At last, they reached the lighthouse poster. The poster was vibrating gently with the sound. Jo picked up one corner and peered into the darkness. The tunnel gaped at her like an invitation.

Allie was almost bug-eyed from the effort of blowing the shell. It was miles harder than it looked in the movies. As she pulled it away from her mouth and gasped for breath, her cousins and Timmy emerged from the tunnel. Allie had never been so pleased to see them in her life.

"Wow!" Max said, staring at the galleon in a daze. "I mean, *way* wow."

"That's what I said," Allie said happily.

Dylan rolled his eyes in mock irritation. "Allie, you're supposed to be looking for *Bodhi*," he joked, "not getting stuck in a buried shipwreck."

"I *found* Bodhi," Allie replied. She waved around the cavern. "He did all this so he could find this ship and steal all the Spanish gold off it."

The teasing look on Dylan's face fell away at the mention of gold. "So you *haven't* just been wasting time . . ." he said, impressed.

They all turned at the sound of singing. It echoed around the cavern like a ghostly siren. Bodhi was coming back.

"*. . . WEY, HEY, BRO THE MAN DOWN . . .*"

There was no time to pull Allie free. Jo seized the conch shell. She and the others scampered off to hide wherever they could.

Bodhi wriggled into the cavern. "You still here?" he grinned at Allie. "Heh-heh." He reached for the next crate. "Any messages while I was gone?" he enquired, hefting the crate into his arms. "Heh-heh. Funny."

Max stepped out from his hiding place. Bodhi was so startled he almost dropped the crate.

"Yeah, we've got a message for you," Max said. He folded his arms as Dylan, Jo and Timmy all stepped into plain view. "You're busted. 'Bro'."

"Whoa," Bodhi said, stumbling backwards. "Harsh." He dropped the crate and turned away. Jo, Max, Dylan and Timmy flew after him. Allie was forced to watch from her hole.

The surfer ran along the deck to the main mast. Like a monkey, he started climbing. Jo, Dylan and Max were undeterred, and shinned up after him, leaving Timmy to bark madly on the deck.

The mast groaned from the extra weight. Four hundred years in the cavern had rotted it through. As Bodhi grabbed a rope to swing back down to the deck, the mast toppled like a felled tree.

"Hang on – we're going for a ride . . ." Jo yelled.

She and the others clung on tightly as the mast collapsed.

"Wooooahhh!"

It stopped inches from the deck. Dylan hopped

off. "In some ways, that was not un-fun," he said, straightening out his T-shirt.

Bodhi was back on the main deck. He grabbed the last crate of gold and hurried towards the mouth of the tunnel. Timmy ran to Allie and pulled her out of the mud with his teeth.

The chase was on!

Chapter Ten

The sun was setting by the time Bodhi came running out of the shack with his crate of gold. Timmy barked, growled and snapped at his heels.

"You want the gold?" Bodhi panted, struggling to run with his heavy load. "Take it – it's heavy."

He dropped the crate and increased his speed. Timmy had to dodge and veer away to avoid getting squashed.

"Rowphhh!" he barked.

Bodhi was now racing towards the ocean, to where a man was tinkering with a jet-ski. He gave him a hefty shove, leaped on to the jet-ski and roared out to sea.

"Hey!" the man shouted, hopping up and down and waving his fists helplessly at the thief.

Max's friendly harbour seal put its face out of the waves to see what was going on. It saw Bodhi thrashing through the waves towards it, and barked happily.

"Leave me alone, flipper-head," Bodhi snarled. He gunned the jet-ski and tried to pass the seal.

But now it was the dolphin's turn to put in an appearance. It leaped out of the water in a blur of slick grey skin and knocked Bodhi off the jet-ski like a ninepin in an extremely wet bowling alley.

"Wahhhh!" Bodhi spluttered, coming up for air.

The seal slapped him smartly with both flippers.

"Heyyyy!" Bodhi complained. "You guys are crazy!"

With the seal and the dolphin both watching him with narrowed eyes, he had no choice. Panicking now, Bodhi turned and swam back to shore. When he reached the sand, he picked himself up and started running.

"He's heading for the Crazy Creature Club!" Dylan shouted.

The Five chased the thieving surf dude towards

Jo and Dylan's magnificently monstrous sand living room. Bodhi dodged among the sofas and armchairs, Timmy herding him expertly towards the centre of the sculpture, where the Kirrins were gathering beside the giant Frankenstein butler figure.

"This is going to hurt him more than it hurts me . . ." Jo sighed, leaning into the sandy Frankenstein and pushing with all her strength.

The others helped. The statue groaned and toppled over on to Bodhi, burying him up to his neck in sand.

"Awfffff!" Bodhi spluttered. He was completely stuck.

"Got some sand down your shorts, huh?" said Dylan, folding his arm and grinning at the hapless villain. "Itches like crazy, doesn't it?"

Later that evening, it was party time down on the beach. The *luau* was in full swing. Flaming torches glimmered along the shoreline. The guests were wearing flower *leis* around their necks, and everything was decorated in Polynesian style.

The Five watched from their position beside

Duke's surf shack. Allie pointed to where Sierra was
dancing with a boy. "Looks like Sierra's gotten over
Bodhi," she said.

As Sierra danced, she kept reaching down to
scratch her legs. The guy she was dancing
with tried to copy her, thinking it was all part of
the dance.

"And she's making the poison ivy work for her,"
Allie continued approvingly. "Good job, Sierra."

A sheriff shouldered his way through the party,
leading Bodhi away in a pair of handcuffs. Bodhi
was still covered in sand.

"One problem with Bodhi going to jail is that Duke's team loses its best surfer," Max remarked.

Jo smiled. "Luckily, it doesn't matter ..." she said, patting the stack of gold crates from the galleon, which stood on the sand beside her. "This gold was on Duke's land – he's rich."

Duke Sonoma himself ambled over to the Five. He was wreathed in smiles, and his white teeth shone in his tanned face. "Thanks, grommets," he drawled. "This gold will let me fix up my shack and buy the whole stretch of beach. I'll keep it just the way it is."

"That's great, Duke," said Max in delight. "Glad we could help."

Allie laughed, and the cousins gave each other high-fives. There was a lot to celebrate tonight.

"Duke, you might want to mention it to Arlene Gundall over there," said Allie, turning back to the old surfer. "She's already measuring for drapes."

Sure enough, Arlene Gundall was on her hands and knees beside the shack. Ignoring the party, she was flicking a tape measure expertly up and down, and side to side.

"My pleasure," Duke grinned.

The Five watched him saunter over to Arlene. "Hey Arlene," they heard him say. "Funny story . . ."

Jo's dad Ravi suddenly appeared, dressed from head to foot in traditional Polynesian costume. "Come on, kids – join the party!" he shouted cheerfully. He waved a strange device at them, with a sword blade at one end and a burning torch at the other. "I'll teach you the sword-fire dance!"

Ravi started enthusiastically twirling the sword-torch around his neck, through his legs and up and in the air. "Ow!" he roared every time a blade or a flame sliced at his skin. Which was rather a lot. "Ow! . . . Ow! . . . Ow! . . . Ow!"

"Thanks, Uncle Ravi," said Allie a little faintly. "Maybe we'll stick with Aunt George . . ."

George was hula-dancing like a thing possessed, shaking her grass-skirted hips and twirling her *lei*.

"Go wild, Mum!" Jo laughed, and jogged over to join in.

As the others started to dance as well, Timmy trotted over to the whispering waves on the shoreline and threw himself down in the cool sand. The harbour seal popped out of the water and barked plaintively at him. Timmy barked back, throwing in a little whine. The dolphin appeared and joined in the conversation with some whistles and chirps of his own. It sounded like they all wished they could dance as well.

Luau music was seriously catchy.

Epilogue

It was Handy Hint time. Jo worked the videocamera this time, pointing it at Dylan as he stood on the beach in a pair of sturdy leather boots.

"Sticky Situation Number Four Hundred and Sixty-Six – You Have To Identify A Rattlesnake," Jo announced.

Dylan stood tall. "First," he informed the camera as the others watched, "if you're in snake country, wear thick, leather boots for protection and stomp loudly – it scares snakes away."

He stomped to illustrate, sending up a little puff of sand as he did so.

"But if you see a snake," he continued, setting his

feet down again, "you need to know if it's dangerous or not."

He walked down the beach to where there was a large sand sculpture of a rattlesnake. Jo tracked him with the camera lens.

"A rattlesnake's head is diamond-shaped, with wide jaws," Dylan said, pointing at these rattlesnake characteristics in the sand. "If you see a snake like that, stay away from it."

He took several steps backward, folded his arms and smiled into the camera. "If you don't bother a snake, it won't bother you," he said. "Then you'll be a Master Outdoorsman like me, Dylan."

An enormous wave hit the shore. Crashing down on Dylan's head, it left him soaked, dazed and covered with seaweed, crabs and an assortment of flopping fish.

"Oooppp – ohhhhhh . . ." Dylan staggered a little, but kept his composure. The others roared with laughter. Jo was having difficulty keeping the camera straight.

"Oh – bonus tip," Dylan added, pulling fish out of his hair. "Never turn your back on the ocean."

Which was advice that maybe Dylan should have taken *before* a second wave came and drenched him all over again.

THE CASE OF THE CACTUS, THE COOT, AND THE COWBOY BOOT

Read on for Chapter One
of the Famous 5's next Case File . . .

*Hodder
Children's
Books*

A division of Hachette Children's Books

Chapter One

The Old Wild West had come to life.

The Kirrin cousins, plus Jo's dog Timmy, stared round at the bank, the saloon, the horse trough and the old wooden verandas that lined the dusty old-fashioned street. If it hadn't been for the assorted rides, colourful stalls and the fact that the horses were made of plastic, they could have slipped back in time.

Allie shifted her backpack to a more comfortable spot on her shoulder. She tossed her blond hair over her shoulders, and leaned in to see what it said on the large, cheery-looking map in front of her.

"Welcome to Scrappy Flapjacks' Cowboy Town!"

she read. "No visit to Los Angeles is complete without it."

It was thanks to Allie that the Kirrins were in the States. Her parents had gone away, leaving Jo's family in charge of the cousins down at Allie's beach house in Malibu. They were making the most of their time in the California sun.

Max pushed his shaggy blond fringe out of his eyes and pointed at the map. "Can we ride the stagecoach?" he said in excitement. "YEEEE-HAAAAAGH!" He coughed a bit. "That actually hurts a little," he confessed sheepishly.

Dylan had found something far more interesting on the map. "We can pan for gold?" he gasped. His glasses started steaming up at the prospect of cash. "That's got my name all over it. Although I'd rather use a really big vacuum cleaner."

Allie turned to consult her third and final cousin. "What do *you* want to do, Jo?" she said.

There was no sign of Jo.

"Jo? . . ." Allie called, looking round in confusion. "Jo?"

Jo had wandered over to a game booth, where you had to shoot a little bow and arrow at balloons to try and pop them. This was more her kind of thing than gold or stagecoach rides.

"I only have to pop three balloons?" Jo was checking with a craggy looking woman dressed in a US Cavalry outfit, who was in charge of the booth. "Why don't you just give me a prize?"

The woman handed Jo the bow and arrows. "Careful, girlie," she said in a patronising tone of voice, "it's not as easy as it—"

THWACK-THWACK-THWACK!

In quick succession, Jo fired the arrows and popped the balloons.

"—looks," the woman finished uncertainly. She shrugged, trying not to look impressed. "Oh, OK, what prize do you want?"

"I wanna horseshoe!" screeched a child, before Jo had a chance to choose something. He pointed his grubby little fingers at the prizes ranged round the booth. "I wanna tepee!"

As he pointed, he knocked over his cup of juice. The sticky purple drink spilled all over the booth's counter. Now his voice rose an octave.

"I spilled my juice," he roared, slapping his hands in the purple mess and sending it everywhere.

"WAAAAGGHHHHH!"

"Hey, buckaroo," said the woman behind the booth, trying desperately to sound cheerful. "Only smiles at Scrappy Flapjacks'! This is a happy— you're getting grape juice everywhere, you pipsqueak!"

With a heavy sigh, she got a cloth and started cleaning up the mess. "Grab a prize, girlie," she told Jo over her shoulder.

Jo's cousins had caught up with her, and they all stared at the choice of prizes. There was a clown in a cowboy hat, a model covered-wagon, a teepee with a clock in it and various soft toys that dangled from the booth's roof.

"So what are you going to take?" asked Allie, pressing in eagerly behind Jo. "The clown with a cowboy hat is nice."

Jo spotted a small ceramic cactus tucked in amongst the prizes. "Mum likes plants," she said, leaning over and taking the cactus. "She'll love getting this when she and Dad get back from Sequoia."

"Can we pan for gold now?" Dylan begged. "I hear it calling to me."

The cousins moved away, joking and laughing. The woman at the booth was still mopping up when a phone started ringing under the counter. She put down her cloth and picked up the phone.

"Hello? . . ." Suddenly her voice dropped down low. "Yeah, I got the component . . ." she said, glancing round to make sure no one was listening. "It's right here, hidden in a cactus . . ."

Still with the phone pressed to her ear, she peered over at the stack of prizes. A look of panic crossed her face. "Where is it?" she muttered. "Where'd it go?"

As she caught sight of Jo carrying the cactus away, her expression hardened.

"Er, little problem with the cactus," she said into the phone, watching as the cousins made their way across Cowboy Town towards the gold-panning area. "But don't worry – I know where it is . . ."

She hung up and watched as Jo put the cactus into her rucksack.

". . . and I'm going to get it back . . ." she said quietly to herself.

THE FAMOUS FIVE'S
SURVIVAL GUIDE

Packed with useful information on surviving outdoors and solving mysteries, here is the one mystery that the Famous Five never managed to solve. See if you can follow the trail to discover the location of the priceless Royal Dragon of Siam.

The perfect book for all fans of mystery, adventure and the Famous Five!

ISBN 9780340970836